Detective Dog

Adaptation by Jamie White

Based on TV series teleplays
written by Raye Lankford and Peter K. Hirsch

Based on characters created by Susan Meddaugh

HOUGHTON MIFFLIN HARCOURT
Boston · New York

For information about permission to reproduce selections from this book, write to Permissions, Houghton Mifflin Harcourt Publishing Company, 215 Park Avenue South, New York, New York 10003.

ISBN: 978-0-547-86021-3 hc
ISBN: 978-0-547-77512-8 pa

Cover design by Rachel Newborn
Book design by Bill Smith Studio

www.hmhbooks.com
www.marthathetalkingdog.com

Manufactured in China
SCP 10 9 8 7 6 5 4 3 2
4500393982

Part One

POOCH ON PATROL

A dog's life is never dull. Especially when you're a talking dog like me, Martha!

Ever since Helen fed me her alphabet soup, I've been able to speak. And speak and speak . . . No one's sure how or why, but the letters in the soup traveled up to my brain instead of down to my stomach.

Now as long as I eat my daily bowl of alphabet soup, I can talk. To my family—Helen, baby Jake, Mom, Dad, and Skits, who only speaks Dog. To Helen's best human friend, T.D. To anyone who'll listen.

Sometimes my family wishes I didn't talk quite so much. But my speaking has come in handy when fighting crime. Like the time I called 911 to catch a burglar. Or when I became a K-9 cop!

Oh, sure, I'd once thought a stakeout was the butcher shop's version of takeout, and the only things I'd pursued were squirrels and garbage trucks. But that was before Helen, Skits, and I bumped into Officer O'Reilly in town. He was with a dog!

Skits and I greeted him with a nice-to-meet-you sniff. But the dog just stood there. "What's the matter with him?" I asked.

"He's on duty," said Officer O'Reilly. "Rascal's part of our K-9 unit."

"You mean he's a police dog?" I asked.

"Yup," he replied. "We're just finishing our beat. Unfortunately, my partner and I are going to be in different cities tomorrow." He puffed out his chest. "There's a big case in Chicago. They need a smart cop to help them crack it."

"You're going to Chicago?" I asked.

"Uh . . . not me," he mumbled, glancing down at Rascal. "I'll be stuck patrolling alone for the next few days."

"You don't have to patrol alone," I said. "I could patrol with you."

Officer O'Reilly didn't look too sure. "Really?"

"Why not?" I asked. "When you patrol, you go around making sure everything is okay, right?"

"Right," he said.

"I'm great at patrolling!" I said. "I patrol my yard all the time. Watch." I paced the sidewalk, looking left and right. "See? I'm patrolling. Nope, no criminals here."

Officer O'Reilly rubbed his chin. "I don't know. Being a K-9 officer requires special training."

"But I'm the police force's secret weapon," I reminded him. "I brought in Louie Kablooie and Jimmy Gimme Moore. I stopped that soup spy ring thingy. And the dogs that were robbing the butcher's!"

To convince him, I showed off my best tricks. I sat, stayed, and played dead. I even begged. "Please? Please let me be a cop! Please please please please PLEASE!"

"Oh, all right," Officer O'Reilly sighed. "Report to the station tomorrow. We start walking the beat at nine o'clock sharp."

Hot dog!

BUGGING OUT

How does a dog learn to be a top K-9 cop? By watching TV's coolest crime-fighting canine, Courageous Collie Carlo! Sigh. He's so dreamy.

I was in the middle of my fourth episode when Helen interrupted. "Can't I watch my show now?" she asked.

"Sorry," I replied. "No time for idle television viewing. I've got to be prepared for my beat tomorrow."

On TV, the officer was making an arrest. "POLICE! FREEZE!" he ordered. *So that's how it's done,* I thought.

All day and night, I watched TV cops bust bad guys. They shouted "POLICE! FREEZE!" 102 more times. Helen had counted.

"TV is not going to teach you how to be a police dog," she groaned.

"How can you say that? Look what I've learned already!" I said, looking tough.

"Yeah, but none of that stuff ever happens. Like that!" said Helen. On TV, a detective had just discovered smuggled pineapples on a train. "No one smuggles stuff into Wagstaff City."

"Smuggling means you sneak something in that isn't supposed to be there, right?" I said. "So maybe people are smuggling things into Wagstaff City all the time."

"I hope not," said Helen. "Especially if it's food. That would be really bad."

I imagined train cars bursting with burgers, hot dogs, and steaks. A real gravy train. Next stop—Martha's belly! "What could ever be bad about food?" I asked dreamily.

"It could be bad if a bug was hiding in it," said Helen.

"What could an itty-bitty bug do?"

Helen looked serious. "Eat all the crops. Or the forest. Especially if there were lots of bugs."

"That's awful!" I agreed.

Helen yawned and rose to go to bed. "Like I said, it'd never happen in Wagstaff City."

"But what if it did?"

"It won't," said Helen, walking away.

"How can you be sure?" I called after her. But she left me to worry. "Just think, Skits," I said. "There could be smuggled food out there right now!" I snuggled into my chair. "I don't know how I'll ever be able to go to slee— *ZZZZZZZZZ.*"

OFFICER MARTHA

The next thing I knew, the sun was shining and I was wearing a police uniform. I was . . . Officer Martha! Oh, yeah. You got that right.

I was a dog on the prowl, cruising the mean city streets in my patrol car. I had a nose for trouble and sniffed out crime by, uh, sniffing. All day, I went above and beyond the smell of duty. Then I hit the doughnut shop with my partner, O'Reilly.

But being a cop wasn't all flashy lights and jelly doughnuts. It was cream-filled doughnuts too. Oh, and bad guys.

14

That morning, I'd spotted a nervous-looking man in an alley. He'd just stepped out of his truck when I approached him.

"Got any smuggled food in there?" I asked.

The man scoffed. "In Wagstaff City?"

"Oh, right," I said. "Silly me. Have a good day!"

But as I walked away, I heard a loud munching sound. I turned around. The man had opened the back of his truck. It was packed with pineapples! And the munching noise seemed to be coming from inside them!

Within seconds, a gang of bugs chewed their way out of the fruit and took to the sky.

"Let's get cracking," snarled their leader. They swooped down onto a field, clearing crops like a giant lawnmower.

Next they hit the neighborhoods and chomped down all the trees. From our yard, my family watched helplessly below a cloud of sawdust. "I was wrong!" cried Helen. "People do smuggle things into Wagstaff City!"

The bugs buzzed off into the distance.

"Martha, look!" Helen exclaimed. "They're swarming Granny's soup factory!"

I watched in horror as the factory began to disappear. How would I say "POLICE! FREEZE!" without soup? How would I say anything?!

"NOOOOOOOOOOOOOOO!" I yelled.

That was when I woke up from my nightmare.

I padded into the kitchen and stretched just as Helen zoomed around the corner. She slammed into me.

"Oops!" she said.

"POLICE! FREEZE!" I shouted.

Helen grinned. "Is there a problem, Officer?"

"Oh, no problem," I said. "Except for a little *speeding!*"

"Sorry," she said, walking slower. "I'm running late for school."

I gave her my sternest look. "I'm going to have to give you a citation."

"Citation?" asked Helen. "You mean, like a piece of paper that says I broke the law? Like a speeding ticket?"

"Afraid so," I said. Then I remembered dogs can't write. Darn paws! "Uh, grab a notepad and write your citation down, would you? Your fine is five bones."

"I'm guessing you don't mean five dollars," said Helen.

"Nope. Five tasty biscuit bones."

Helen added them to Mom's shopping list. Duty done, I yawned.

"What's the matter?" Helen asked. "Up late fighting crime, Officer Martha?"

"I couldn't sleep," I said, pacing. "I was worrying about smuggled food."

"Martha," said Helen slowly, "there's no smuggling in Wagstaff City."

"But what if there were?"

Helen giggled.

"This is serious!" I said. "The security of our food is at stake."

"It sure is," said Helen, looking at something behind me. I spun around to catch Skits about to eat my soup.

"POLICE! FREEZE!" I said. "Step away from the bowl!"

A police dog's job is never done.

THE SMELL OF DUTY

At nine o'clock, Officer O'Reilly and I began walking our beat. I told him what was on my mind.

"Smuggling?" he said. "Never happens in Wagstaff City."

"How can you be sure?" I asked.

"Because planes and boats from other countries don't come here," he answered.

I thought this over as we reached the seaport. A crane was unloading crates from a ship while the captain and his first mate looked on.

"Morning," said Officer O'Reilly, tipping his hat to them.

I sniffed the air. "Wait a minute! I smell a rat."

The captain looked nervous, but Officer O'Reilly smiled. "Of course you do," he said. "We're at the dock. It's loaded with rats."

"No," I said. "I mean, something doesn't smell right. It smells like . . . rutabagas."

"R-rutabagas?" the captain stuttered. "Oh, uh, not around here. We don't have those."

Oh yeah? I thought. Then why is that rat behind you carrying a . . . RUTABAGA?!

My ears perked up. *And what's that munching sound?* I wondered. But there was no time to find out. I pounced in front of the rat. "POLICE! FREEZE!"

"Squeak!" went the criminal. It fled across the dock, but I was right on its tail.

"Martha, leave it!" cried Officer O'Reilly.

The rat scurried under a forklift moving a crate. I leaped over it. At the sight of me, the driver's mouth dropped. The forklift swerved. And—*CRASH!*—the crate smashed to the dock.

"Officer Martha! Heel!" shouted Officer O'Reilly.

The three men chased me, but I wouldn't stop tailing that rat.

Suddenly, the rat dropped the rutabaga and darted into the crack of a door. "Come out with your hands—I mean, paws—up!" I ordered.

Officer O'Reilly and the others limped up behind me. "Martha!" he said. "There's nothing in there."

"You're right," I said. "It's in his pocket!"

Officer O'Reilly turned as purple as a rutabaga. He yanked my collar. "I have to apologize for my partner," he said. "It's her first day on the beat. Come on, Martha. Let's go."

"But I'm telling you," I said as we walked away, "something smells fishy!"

"Of course it's fishy," he snapped. "You're by the river. The river is full of fish."

"Not that kind of fishy."

But Officer O'Reilly just shook his head.

BYE-BYE, BONES

"Fired?" I cried. "You can't fire me."

The chief frowned at me. "I have no choice," he said. "K-9 cops can't chase rats on the beat. It's a matter of security. People could've been hurt."

"But I wasn't chasing the rat!" I protested. "I was chasing the food the rat was carrying."

"K-9 officers don't eat on the beat either," said Officer O'Reilly.

"I wasn't going to eat it," I said. "It's a root vegetable, after all. It's not a sausage. I was going to inspect it."

The men exchanged doubtful glances.

"Come on," I pleaded. "You're not really going to fire me, are you?"

Oh, but they did.

• • • • •

"I can't believe I got fired, Skits," I said. "How many jobs have I had? Fire dog, radio host, telemarketer . . . I've never been fired from any of them."

I bet Helen won't pay her speeding ticket when she finds out I'm not a cop anymore, I thought. *Bye-bye, bones.*

Just then, a truck drove past us. I sniffed.

"Hey!" I said, bolting up. "It's that smell again."

Woof? barked Skits.

"The smell from the docks," I explained. "It's coming from that truck. Follow me!"

Skits and I tracked the scent into town. It led us to an alley littered with trash cans.

33

We crept closer. "The captain!" I gasped as the truck's doors opened. "Quick, Skits! Hide!"

We dove into a pile of trash. Just a few feet away, the captain and first mate met by the back of the truck.

"That dog almost blew our cover," said the captain.

"Yeah," said his partner. "I thought we were done for when she nosed out that rutabaga."

"Lucky for us," said the captain, "people think there's no smuggling in Wagstaff City."

"Heh-heh," the men laughed.

"Skits," I whispered. "Those rutabagas might be risky! We've got tell the police!"

REPORTING RISKY RUTABAGAS

At the police station, the chief and Officer O'Reilly looked weary.

"Thanks for the tip," said the chief. "Run on home now, Martha."

No way, I thought. *If those crooks aren't stopped, who knows what they'll smuggle next? Tons of turnips? Boatloads of beets? Countless crates of cabbage?! Blech.*

"NO!" I cried. "Something smells rotten, I tell you!"

He pinched his nose. "Maybe it's you."

"Oh, uh, that," I mumbled. "I had to take cover in some garbage. Listen! THERE'S SOMETHING WRONG WITH THOSE RUTABAGAS!"

"Okay, okay!" the chief sighed. "O'Reilly, go check it out or she'll never stop hounding us."

"I am not a hound," I said, offended. "But I am part pit bull."

Officer O'Reilly shook his head. "Not *hound* as in a dog breed. *Hound* as in you're bugging us."

"That's it!" I cried. "Bugs! They're in the rutabagas. I heard them chewing!"

I ran out the door.

Skits and Officer O'Reilly followed me back to the alley. Sure enough, the truck was still there.

The captain and first mate met with a jumpy-looking guy. We couldn't hear what they were saying. But we could see the captain open the back of his truck. Inside were oodles of rutabagas!

"Well, what do you know?" Officer O'Reilly whispered.

Why isn't he arresting them? I wondered. *What's he waiting for?*

Then he turned to me. "Ready, partner?"

My tail wagged in excitement. "Really? I get to say it?"

Officer O'Reilly nodded.

In one leap, I popped out from behind the trash can. "POLICE!" I shouted. "FREEZE!"

The men jumped in surprise. Their rutabaga-smuggling days were over, thanks to . . . Officer Martha! Give that dog a bone.

The next morning, Officer O'Reilly apologized to me as we left the station. "Sorry I didn't believe you."

"It's okay," I said.

"If those bugs had gotten loose, no telling what damage they could've done," he said. "You deserve a medal."

"A medal would be nice, but I can think of something better," I hinted. Because what's the next best thing to taking a bite out of crime? Taking a bite out of a sweet, tasty doughnut.

Later, I told Helen all about it. "Officer O'Reilly said it was the perfect reward for protecting the security of our entire food chain."

Woof? barked Skits.

"*Security* means keeping something safe," I answered. "Like when we bark at strangers to keep the house secure."

"That reminds me," said Helen. "I still owe you for my citation."

I love being a cop!

With the smugglers behind bars, Wagstaff City was safe once again. At least, for a little while . . .

Part Two
MEET SPARKY

"Curious Crystal was in a pickle, all right! The 3:10 from Piscataway would be barreling down the tracks in a jiff. The girl detective was in trouble."

Helen stopped reading. "A detective is someone whose job is to find out things, like clues, to solve a mystery," she said.

Helen kept reading.

"She gave Winky the secret danger whistle! Winky's ears went up. 'Bow wow!' he bellowed, and leapt out the window."

"Dogs don't go 'bow wow,'" I said. "We 'woof,' we 'arf,' we 'yip'—but 'bow wow'? I've never heard it."

"Martha, can't we finish the book?"

"Go on. I'm loving it," I said. "I'm on the edge of my tail."

"*Winky raced to the train tracks, chewed through the ropes, and freed Curious Crystal! They hightailed it to the police station with the evidence. In minutes, Inspector Pinkus had caught Carnation Kelly red-handed! Curious Crystal and Winky had put a stop to the Carnation Caper!*"

Helen closed the book. "The end."

"I don't get it," I said. "That Kelly guy was stealing capes? I thought he was after the diamonds."

"Not a cape. A caper," said Helen, lifting a box of books onto her bed. "A caper is a plan to try to steal something or commit a crime. Each of these books is about a different caper. *Curious Crystal and the Emerald Crab Caper, Curious Crystal and the Mysterious Cottage Caper*..."

She stared at the covers. "I wish I were a kid who solved mysteries."

"You'd be great!" I said. "You could be Heroic Helen and I'd be Sparky, your crime-sniffing sidekick."

"Okay," said Helen. "But first we need a mystery, Sparky."

I suggested we try the kitchen first. The mysteries would taste better.

"Look for anything strange and I'll write it down," she said.

I stopped in my tracks. "Look at that calendar! Tomorrow's date is circled in red!"

"So?" said Helen.

"It could be the date a crime is going to be committed. By . . . the Red Heart Gang!"

"That's *our* calendar," said Helen. "I don't think any criminals use our calendar to plan their crimes."

Then I noticed a tastier clue.

"Crumbs! Let's follow them."

I licked them up as I went.

Mmm. Detective work is delicious!

"Martha," said Helen, "there are no mysteries here. And even if there were, you'd be eating the evidence."

"I'm trying to find out what the criminal stole," I said, licking my chops. "I think it's apple cobbler."

The trail ended at my chair. "Aha! And the master thief was sitting in my chair— Oh!" I giggled, remembering my morning snack. "Actually, it was peach cobbler."

"Let's go outside before we discover what else the master thief stole," Helen suggested.

THE WHISTLER'S WARNING

"Hey, this might be something!" said Helen, picking a business card off the sidewalk. "Someone must have dropped it."

On the card was a picture of a top hat, mustache, and monocle, as well as a name. "The Whistler," read Helen. "Who do you think that is?"

"Someone who whistles?" I asked.

You've Been Warned!!

Helen flipped over the card and gasped.

I ran in panicked circles.

"Who's been warned? Are *we* being warned? What about? What's going to happen to us?"

"Beats me. But Heroic Helen and Sparky are going to find out."

"Do we have to?" I asked.

"Yes," said Helen, examining the card. "The handwriting is distinctive. This is our first clue."

While she slipped it into her notebook, I sniffed a trail of muddy footprints on the sidewalk. "Is this another clue?" I asked.

"Weird," said Helen. "There's only the print of the right shoe. It's almost as if whoever made it was hopping."

"Maybe the Whistler is a hopper!" I said.

"Whoever made this footprint is going that way," said Helen. "Let's pursue it, Sparky!"

"W-w-wait a minute," I said, shuddering. "That footprint is huge. It could be a monster! Can't we pursue the hopping Whistler from home?"

"That wouldn't be a pursuit," said Helen. "If you pursue someone, you follow them so you can catch them."

"Okay," I said. "But I liked it better when we were pursuing the peach cobbler."

Helen and I followed the prints until they grew too faint to see. "The mud must be wearing off the sole," she sighed. "We've lost the trail."

Suddenly, we heard a loud, squelchy *THUD!*
It sounded like a giant. A *hopping* giant!

"It's him!" Helen shouted. "Hide!"

We dove into the bushes.

THUD! *THUD!* *THUD!*

"He's getting closer!" I whispered. My heart
beat faster as I imagined the one-footed giant
stomping us flat. Slowly, we peeked out of
the bushes.

"T.D.!" Helen cried.

"Aaaagh!" yelled T.D. as we popped out of the bushes.

"Aha!" I said. "*You* were making the footprint, so you're the Whistler! Who are you warning and what are you warning them about?"

"Huh?" he said.

"He's not the Whistler," said Helen. "T.D., what are you doing with that thing?"

"I got this mop stuck in my dad's boot," he said. "I thought walking around might loosen it up. Here, give me a hand."

"Nggh!" groaned T.D., straining in effort. "Who's the Whistler, anyway?"

"We don't know yet," I said. "We're going to find out."

POP! The boot came off, sending T.D. and Helen flying onto their bottoms. Mud splattered everywhere.

"Yeah," said Helen, frowning at her mud-soaked pants. "Right after Heroic Helen changes her clothes."

THE MYSTERIOUS MAN

Helen crossed out something in her notebook:

"There goes that clue," she said. "It was a red herring."

I raised my head from the water bowl. "Red herring?" I said. "I thought it was a mop in a boot."

"A red herring is something that throws detectives off the trail. It seems like a clue, but it's not."

"How many clues do we have left in the notebook?" I asked.

"Just one," said Helen, pulling out the business card. "There's no way we're going to find out who the Whistler is from this."

"Something's bound to turn up," I said.

Helen picked a piece of paper off the ground. "Litter!" she muttered. "People should clean up after themselves."

Then she read it. "Hey, it's a list of stores!"

"Flower shop," read Helen. "That's where Mom works! And this handwriting looks familiar."

Just then, a gloved hand reached out and snatched the list. A man with a thin mustache towered over us. He wore a suit with a carnation tucked into his lapel.

"Excuse me," he said. "But I believe that is mine. I dropped it when I was getting a yogurt."

The mysterious man turned to leave, but stopped. "Do you happen to know the way to the flower shop?" he asked.

"It's two blocks down and make a left," I told him.

"A talking dog," he murmured. "How curious. Much obliged." Then he put on his top hat and walked away.

Helen stared after him. "Martha!" she cried. "When was the last time you saw someone wearing a monocle and top hat in Wagstaff City?"

"Well, there's that guy on the peanut jar, and then there's that card we found—" I gasped. "He could be the Whistler!"

"Let's follow him!" said Helen.

But the man had vanished.

"He must be headed to the flower shop," said Helen. "If we hurry, we can beat him there."

Heroic Helen and Sparky took off in hot pursuit.

THE GENTLEMAN

At the flower shop, Helen and I hid behind large vases of flowers. "This is the perfect camouflage," she whispered.

"Huh?" I said.

"Camouflage is something you use to hide by blending into your background," she explained.

I nodded. "The Whistler will *never* find us—"

Just then, Mom gathered a bunch of our camouflage to fill an order.

"Mom, you're ruining our stake-out!" Helen said.

"Steak? Out?" I asked, popping up. "Steak out where?"

Helen giggled. "A stakeout is when you hide and wait for someone to show up so you can see what they're doing. Like if they're up to no good.

"Mom," she said. "We need to have a stakeout if we're going to catch a criminal."

"What criminal?" Mom asked.

"He wears a top hat and monocle and he's called the Whistler," I said.

Mom smiled. "Ooh, he sounds terrifying!"

"We're not positive he's a criminal," I said, "but he did want to know where the flower shop was."

"Well," said Mom, "if a man in a top hat and monocle comes by and tries to whistle at me, I'll let you know. In the meantime, could you pick up a chicken for dinner tomorrow?"

Helen wasn't happy about taking a break from our stakeout. But I suggested we move it to Karl's Butcher Shop and have real steak with it.

Sadly, that didn't happen. But Karl did toss me some brisket for being his last customer. "I'll lock up behind you," he said, following us to the door. "Since those recent robberies in the neighborhood, you can't be too careful."

"Robberies?" I asked. "What robberies?"

"Didn't you hear?" said Karl. "The dry cleaner, grocery store . . . I was robbed last week. And it was right after my birthday, too. Talk about a birthday surprise."

"Do the police have any idea who it might be?" asked Helen.

"No," said Karl. "But they're calling him the Gentleman. A witness said that the robber was very well dressed."

Then he waved goodbye and locked up.

"Whew!" I said. "I was afraid Karl was going to say that they're looking for someone called the Whistler."

"But what if the Whistler *is* the Gentleman?" said Helen. "He was well dressed, remember? Hmm. This is all going in the notebook. I just know that guy is up to something."

A SOGGY STAKEOUT

The next day, it rained on cats and dogs. Helen and I kept an eye on the flower shop from across the street. We hid behind some bushes.

"Why can't we have the stakeout inside like we did yesterday?" I asked.

"It's easier to run to the police from here," said Helen. "As soon as we see him, you hotfoot it to the station."

Her eyes widened. *"There he is!"*

The Whistler stopped outside the store.

"What if he just wants to buy some flowers?" I asked.

"Then why isn't he going inside?" Helen said.

We watched him whip out his pocket watch, accidentally sending a sheet of paper to the sidewalk. Forget calling him the Whistler. He was more like Professor Butterfingers.

He peeked into the store window. As soon as Mom appeared, he ducked and darted away.

"Okay, that did look suspicious," I admitted.

"He must have thought that Mom saw him," Helen said. "I bet he comes back later. Now's our chance. Get the police!"

"I'm on it!" I said.

I beat paws to the station while Helen went to tell Mom that help was coming. On the way, she picked up the paper that the Whistler had dropped. It was sheet music.

"You've been warned!" read Helen. "Music and lyrics by Mack Guffin. Huh?"

"Helen!" called her Dad.

She looked up to see him.

"What are you doing here?" he asked nervously. "Mr. Guffin hasn't shown up yet, has he?"

"Mr. Guffin? Who's that?" asked Helen.

"I'd show you his card, but I lost it."

"Is this it?" asked Helen, holding up the Whistler's card.

"You found it!" Dad exclaimed. He peered into the shop window before whispering, "It's an anniversary surprise. I don't want your mother to see us."

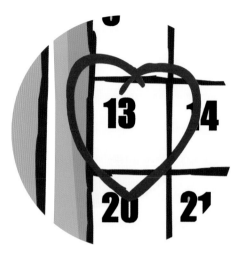

"So that's why there was a red heart on the calendar!" said Helen.

Meanwhile, I was at the police station.

"Let me get this straight," said the chief. "A man in a top hat and monocle named the Whistler is planning to rob the flower shop?"

"Right," I said. "Although he could also be calling himself the Gentleman."

"The Gentleman, eh?" said the chief. "And why should we take your word for this?"

"Because I helped you put away Louie Kablooie and Jimmy Gimme Moore? And the spy ring with those crooks who broke into the museum? And the rutabaga smugglers and—Seriously, do I really have to go through this every time?"

The chief turned to Officer O'Reilly. "She's got a point," he said. "All right, we'll check it out."

THE CROONING CROOK CAPER

While I was convincing the chief and Officer O'Reilly that something funny was going on at the flower shop, Helen was still there, talking to the Whistler.

"I hope we didn't mess things up," she said, handing him his sheet music.

He smiled. "Not at all. I had no idea I was being followed. You're quite the detective," he said. "Well, time to work."

"Can I help you with something?" Mom asked.

"Are you Mariela Lorraine?" asked the Whistler.

"Yes," Mom answered.

He opened his mouth to sing. The chief and I arrived just at that moment, but Helen blocked us at the door. "Wait," she whispered before Officer O'Reilly could say a word. "It's just a surprise for Mom, not a robbery."

Dad gave the Whistler the thumbs-up. At last, the Whistler began to sing.

"Your love I shall pursue," he crooned to Mom. "I'll stick to you like glue. Darling, you've been warned!"

Then he whistled a tune and ended with "Happy anniversary!"

Mom ran into Dad's arms. "Oh, Danny!" she cried. "You remembered!"

"See?" said the chief. "It's just a man who delivers singing telegrams."

"Wait a minute," said Helen, opening her notebook. "Could you tell me what stores have been robbed recently?"

The Chief listed them. "The butcher shop, the grocery store, and the dry cleaner. Why?"

"Did someone in all those places recently celebrate something, like a birthday?" Helen asked.

He shrugged. "You got me."

"Well," said Helen, "Karl at the butcher shop had a birthday. I wonder if he and the other stores got singing telegrams the day they were robbed. I think the Whistler *is* the Gentleman!"

"Hey, look!" I cried, spotting him. "He's unlocking the window!"

"That's how he did it!" said Helen. "He opened the windows at all the stores while he was delivering singing telegrams, so he could break in later!"

The Whistler made a mad dash for the door. But I beat him to it. *Grr,* I growled. "POLICE! FREEZE!"

A little while later, the Whistler was singing a new tune—the jailhouse blues.

"Oh, drat," he said, as the cell doors slammed on him.

"Well, Helen, you were right," said Officer O'Reilly.

"It was the handwriting that tipped me off," she said. "This is what the Whistler gave Dad to tell him what song he was going to sing for Mom's anniversary.

"And," she added, pointing to the Whistler's list of stores, "those are the places he robbed. The handwriting matches."

Officer O'Reilly shook her hand. "Great detective work, Helen!"

Case closed, we headed home. "We did it, Sparky," said Helen. "We solved the Crooning Crook Caper!"

"Bow wow, Heroic Helen," I said. "Bow wow."

How many words do you remember from the story?

beat: the route a police officer patrols

camouflage: what you wear to hide by blending into your background

caper: a plan to steal something or commit a crime

citation: a piece of paper that says someone broke the law

criminal: someone who commits a crime

detective: someone whose job is to discover clues to solve a mystery

monocle: an eyeglass for just one eye

patrol: to go around making sure everything is okay

pursue: to follow someone so you can catch them

security: actions taken to keep something safe

smuggle: to illegally sneak something into a place

stakeout: the act of hiding and waiting for people to show up so you can spy on them

Psst . . . What's the Secret Word?

For this game, you'll need three players—a CLUE-GIVER and two DETECTIVES. Without showing the others, the clue-giver writes the vocabulary words on an index card. These are the secret words!

The clue-giver will offer a one-word clue for the detectives to guess the secret word. (The clue-giver may give up to five clues per word.) The first detective to guess correctly gets a point. The first detective to earn five points wins!

You Have the Right to
Remain Silent

Martha loves to talk . . . except when playing charades. Write the vocabulary words on small pieces of paper and divide them among the players. Without talking, take turns acting out the words. Each correct guess gets a point.

Police! Freeze!

Martha issues Helen a citation for speeding. Pretend you're a K-9 cop and create your own citations for family and friends. For example, you might give your brother a citation for wearing stinky socks. You can also design medals for good behavior. (Jelly doughnuts make good rewards too!)